TEN OF THE BEST MYTHS, LEGENDS & FOLK STORIES

TEN OF THE BEST
ANIMAL MYTHS

DAVID WEST

Crabtree Publishing Company
www.crabtreebooks.com

Crabtree Publishing Company
www.crabtreebooks.com
1-800-387-7650

Publishing in Canada
616 Welland Ave.
St. Catharines, ON
L2M 5V6

Published in the United States
PMB 59051, 350 Fifth Ave.
59th Floor,
New York, NY

Published in **2015 by CRABTREE PUBLISHING COMPANY.**

Printed in the U.S.A./092014/JA20140811

Created and produced by:
David West Children's Books

Project development, design, and concept:
David West Children's Books

Author and designer: David West

Illustrator: David West

Contributing Editor: Steve Parker

Editor: Kathy Middleton

Proofreader: Wendy Scavuzzo

Production coordinator and Prepress technicians:
Samara Parent, Margaret Amy Salter

Print coordinator: Katherine Berti

Library and Archives Canada Cataloguing in Publication

West, David, 1956-, author
    Ten of the best animal myths / David West.

(Ten of the best : myths, legends & folk stories)
Includes index.
Issued in print and electronic formats.
ISBN 978-0-7787-0820-9 (bound).--ISBN 978-0-7787-0807-0 (pbk.).--
ISBN 978-1-4271-7740-7 (pdf).--ISBN 978-1-4271-7732-2 (html)

    1. Tales. I. Title. II. Title: Animal myths.

PZ8.1.W37An 2014   j398.24'5   C2014-903845-3
                                                 C2014-903846-1

Library of Congress Cataloging-in-Publication Data

West, David, 1956-
Ten of the best animal myths / David West.
    pages cm -- (Ten of the best: myths, legends & folk stories)
 Includes index.
 ISBN 978-0-7787-0820-9 (reinforced library binding) --
ISBN 978-0-7787-0807-0 (pbk.) --
ISBN 978-1-4271-7740-7 (electronic pdf) --
ISBN 978-1-4271-7732-2 (electronic html)
1. Tales. 2. Animals--Folklore. [1. Folklore. 2. Animals--Folklore.] I.
Title.

PZ8.1.W4885Ten 2014
398.24'52--dc23
[E]
                                  2014022859

THE STORIES

Anansi the Spider

*This is the story of how Anansi, the **trickster**, came to own all of the stories in the whole world.*

Long ago, all the stories in the world belonged to the sky god, Nyame. Anansi the Spider had long wanted to own them, and one day he offered to buy them.

"I am happy to sell you my stories, Anansi, but my price is high," said Nyame. "You must bring me Mmoboro the hornet, Onini the python, and also Osebo the leopard."

Anansi set to work right away. First he approached Mmoboro the hornet's nest carrying an empty **gourd** with a small hole in it. Sprinkling water over the nest, he shouted: "It is raining and your fragile nest will soon be destroyed! Quick, fly into this dry gourd and save yourself." At once, the hornet flew into the gourd—and Anansi plugged the hole with mud.

To capture the python, Anansi cut a stout pole and walked past Onini's house. Speaking to himself loudly so that Onini could hear, he declared: "My wife is very silly. She says he is shorter, but I say he is longer."

"Who are you talking about?" asked Onini.

"Oh! It's only a silly argument I was having with Mrs. Anansi. She thinks you are shorter than this pole."

"Well, we can soon find the truth if I lie beside it," replied Onini. But he could not make himself straight enough.

"Let me tie one end of you to the pole," said Anansi. "That should help." And so, in this manner and without realizing, Onini was gradually tied to the pole until he could no longer move.

To capture the leopard, Anansi dug a deep pit across a path that Osebo used. He covered the pit with palm leaves. Osebo fell in and cried with terror.

Anansi ran to a log overlooking the pit. "Anansi, help me!" shouted Osebo.

"Tie this rope around you," advised Anansi, as he spun a thick strand of spider's thread. Soon the leopard was entangled in Anansi's web. Anansi hauled him up and took all three captives to Nyame. The price was paid.

This is how Anansi bought ownership of all the world's stories and tales. So, the next time you hear a story—remember where it came from.

Wenebojo and Buffalo

This is the story of how Buffalo (the North American bison) got his great shoulder hump.

Long, long ago, Buffalo did not have a hump. In the summer, he would race across the prairie for fun. Fox ran before him and yelled at all the little animals to get out of the way. But the baby birds in their ground nests could not fly yet. They were trampled and their nests were destroyed.

Each time the birds cried out and told Buffalo not to trample on their nests. But he did not listen, and kept destroying their babies.

Wenebojo heard the birds crying. He saw Fox and Buffalo running across the prairie, causing mayhem.

Buffalo provided food and clothing for the Plains Indians.

Wenebojo ran ahead and stopped Buffalo and Fox in their tracks. With his spear, he hit Buffalo hard across the shoulders. At once, Buffalo hung his head and hunched his shoulders, afraid of the spear and expecting that Wenebojo might hit him again.

"You should be ashamed," scolded Wenebojo. "That's right, Buffalo. Hang your head and raise your shoulders. From this day, you will always have a hump on your shoulders and always carry your head low because of your shame."

Fox slunk away and dug a hole in which to hide. But Wenebojo saw him and said: "You, Fox, will always live in a hole in the ground for not saving the birds."

And that is why the buffalo has a shoulder hump, and why the fox lives in a hole in the ground.

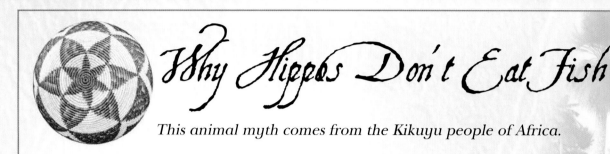

Why Hippos Don't Eat Fish

This animal myth comes from the Kikuyu people of Africa.

When the creator god Lord N'gai made the animals, he created an animal of the forests and plains called the hippopotamus.

The hippopotamus was greedy. Finding plenty of food all around him and no enemies, he ate and ate. And as he ate, he grew fatter and fatter. The fatter he grew, the more he suffered from the heat of the midday sun.

Each day, he walked down to the river to drink. "Oh, how I would like to be like N'gai's little fishes and live in the cool refreshing water," he thought. So, on one particularly hot day, he went to N'gai and asked him, "Please, Lord N'gai, may I become one of the creatures that lives in the rivers and lakes?"

The Kikuyu are a group of Bantu people that live in Southeast Africa.

The good Lord N'gai refused the hippo's wish, afraid that he would eat all his fishes, which were very dear to him.

"I promise that I will not eat your fishes," said the hippo. "I will lie in the river by day and eat along its banks at night."

"How will I know that you will not eat them?" Lord N'gai asked.

"Each night I will spread my dung upon the earth so that you may see that there are no fish bones in it," said the hippo.

Lord N'gai agreed and the hippopotamus kept its promise. This is why the hippo does not eat fish and why it comes out of the water at night to scatter its dung and feed on the vegetation along the banks by its home.

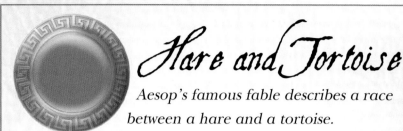

Hare and Tortoise

Aesop's famous fable describes a race between a hare and a tortoise.

Once upon a time, there was a hare who boasted how fast he could run. He was forever teasing Tortoise for his slowness. But one day, Tortoise answered back.

"Who do you think you are? I'll not deny you are swift, but even you can be beaten!"

Hare laughed. "Beaten in a race? Not by you, surely?"

Annoyed by Hare's **bragging**, Tortoise accepted the challenge. The animals planned a lengthy course for the race. The next day at dawn, the two rivals stood at the start line, ready to go.

Hare yawned sleepily as Tortoise plodded off slowly. In fact, when Hare saw how slow Tortoise was, he decided to take a nap.

"Take your time, Tortoise!" shouted Hare. "I'll just grab a nap of forty winks and catch up in a jiffy, old boy."

Much later, Hare suddenly woke up—still at the start! He gazed around, looking for Tortoise. The Sun was sinking down towards the horizon. Tortoise, who had been plodding along since morning, was very close to the finish line.

Hare leaped up and bounded at great speed along the course, trailing a cloud of dust. The finish line was in sight! But it was too late—Tortoise had beaten him. The animals cheered loudly.

Poor Hare! Tired and in disgrace, he slumped down. Tortoise came up beside him, smiled widely and remarked: "Listen, Hare, don't brag about your speed. Slow and steady is all you need!"

Aesop was an ancient Greek slave who wrote a collection of stories we know as Aesop's Fables. It is said that he used his cleverness to acquire his freedom and become an adviser to kings.

Gods and Cats

This Chinese myth explains why cats cannot speak, but humans can.

When the world was a new place, the gods decided to appoint one group of creatures to make sure that everything ran smoothly—especially by keeping an eye on all other animals.

The gods selected the thoughtful, wise-looking cats. The cats were given the power of speech so they could talk with the gods. They were told to report regularly to them about how the world was going.

The cats, however, were simply not interested in the responsibilities given to them by the gods. They were far happier sleeping beneath the cherry trees and playing with the falling blossoms.

After a while, the gods appeared and called the cats.

*Cats were probably **domesticated** around 5,300 years ago in China. They helped keep the farmers' grain free from rats.*

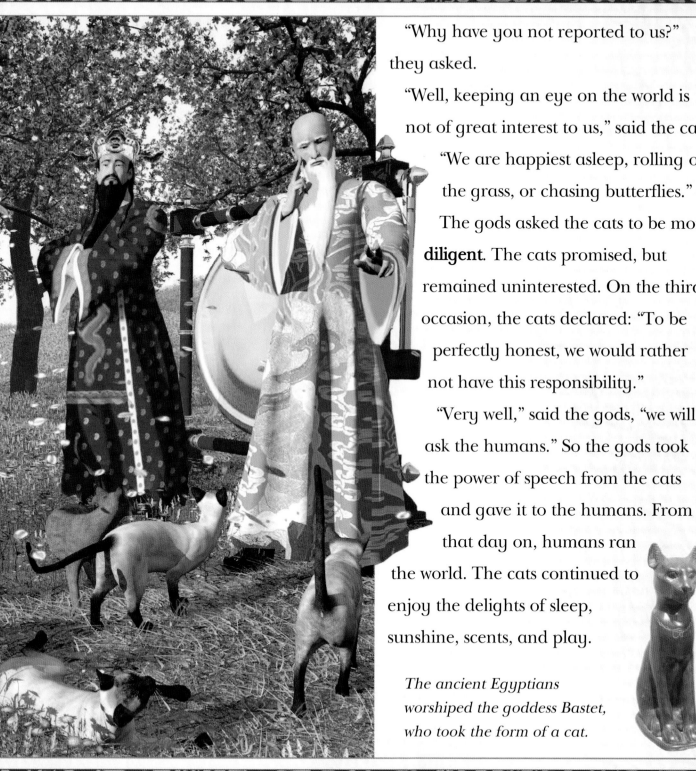

"Why have you not reported to us?" they asked.

"Well, keeping an eye on the world is not of great interest to us," said the cats. "We are happiest asleep, rolling on the grass, or chasing butterflies."

The gods asked the cats to be more **diligent**. The cats promised, but remained uninterested. On the third occasion, the cats declared: "To be perfectly honest, we would rather not have this responsibility."

"Very well," said the gods, "we will ask the humans." So the gods took the power of speech from the cats and gave it to the humans. From that day on, humans ran the world. The cats continued to enjoy the delights of sleep, sunshine, scents, and play.

The ancient Egyptians worshiped the goddess Bastet, who took the form of a cat.

Androclus and the Lion

This account from ancient Rome recalls how a slave and a lion became best friends.

One day in ancient Rome, the crowds were being entertained in the Colosseum. Lions were let loose among unarmed slaves to rip them to pieces. One of the slaves was Androclus of Dacia.

A fearsome lion approached Androclus—and suddenly stopped, wondering what to do. The lion then padded toward the slave, nuzzled his face, and licked his hands. Androclus recovered his **composure** and appeared to recognize the lion. He stroked it, and the spectators applauded and cheered.

The Emperor demanded to know the cause of such a strange event and called the slave to him.

Androclus explained that his master, the **Proconsul** in Africa, was cruel and beat him daily. So Androclus ran away and hid in a cave in the wilderness. Soon afterward, a lion entered the cave, groaning with pain. One of its paws was wounded and bloody. Androclus was, of course, terrified. Yet the lion lay down and stretched out its wounded paw.

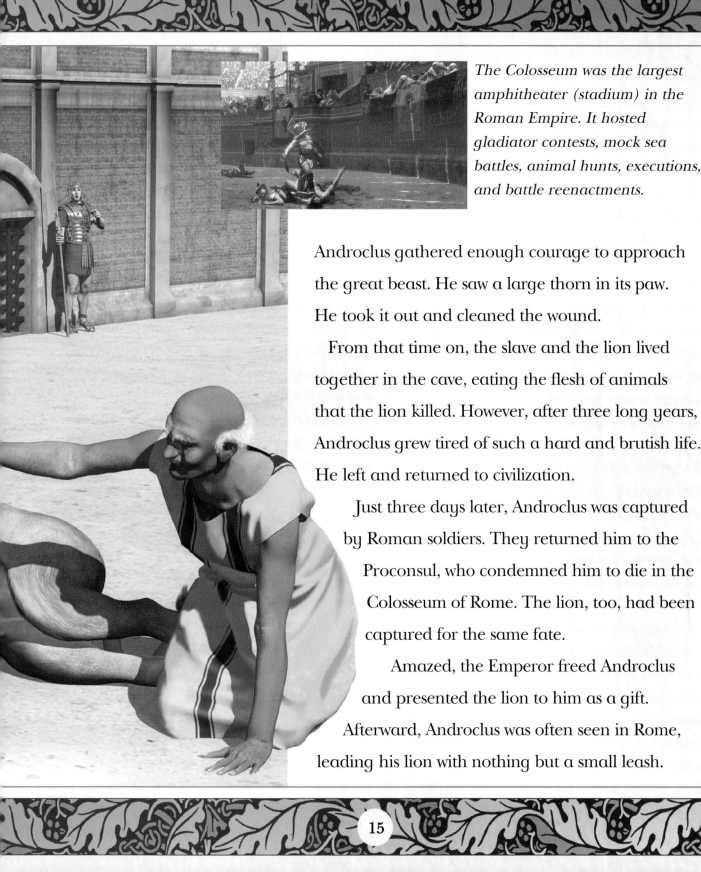

The Colosseum was the largest amphitheater (stadium) in the Roman Empire. It hosted gladiator contests, mock sea battles, animal hunts, executions, and battle reenactments.

Androclus gathered enough courage to approach the great beast. He saw a large thorn in its paw. He took it out and cleaned the wound.

From that time on, the slave and the lion lived together in the cave, eating the flesh of animals that the lion killed. However, after three long years, Androclus grew tired of such a hard and brutish life. He left and returned to civilization.

Just three days later, Androclus was captured by Roman soldiers. They returned him to the Proconsul, who condemned him to die in the Colosseum of Rome. The lion, too, had been captured for the same fate.

Amazed, the Emperor freed Androclus and presented the lion to him as a gift. Afterward, Androclus was often seen in Rome, leading his lion with nothing but a small leash.

Turtle and Peacock

This is a story from ancient India about how a turtle outwits a greedy hunter.

Turtle and Peacock were great friends. They met every day on a riverbank. After a drink of water, Peacock danced near the river and displayed his bright plumage for the amusement of his friend.

One day, a hunter caught Peacock and prepared to take him away to the market. The unhappy bird begged his captor: "Please let me say good-bye to my friend, Turtle. It could be the last time we might ever meet."

The hunter agreed. At the riverbank, Turtle said to the hunter: "If I give you an expensive present, will you let my friend go?"

"Certainly," answered the hunter, whereupon Turtle dived into the water. A few seconds later, he came up with a beautiful pearl. He presented this to the hunter, who immediately released Peacock.

Pearls found in fresh water grow inside **mussels**.

Not long after, the hunter returned. He told Turtle that the price for releasing his friend was not enough. The hunter threatened to catch Peacock again unless he received another pearl. But, on Turtle's advice, Peacock had already fled.

"Well," said Turtle, "I believe that I can get another pearl just like it. Give it to me, and I will dive deep and find an exact match."

The hunter handed over his pearl. Turtle dived into the river—and never returned.

Peacocks are native to India. In Hindu culture, Lord Karthikeya, the god of war, rides a peacock.

Mainu the Frog

This story from Africa tells how a frog ended up marrying the daughter of the Sun and Moon.

One day, a young man named Kimana decided to marry the daughter of the Sun and Moon. He asked each animal in turn if they could take a letter to heaven with his request. But none of the animals knew how to get there.

At last, Mainu the Frog went to Kimana's house, saying he could take the letter to heaven. "A frog?" exclaimed Kimana. "How can you get to heaven when even those with wings cannot?"

"I know the way and they do not," replied Mainu.

Kimana gave Mainu the letter. The frog hid in a well. That night, maidens from heaven climbed down to Earth on a magic web made by the Great Spider. They filled the jugs they were carrying with water from the well. Secretly, Mainu jumped into one of the jugs.

The maidens climbed back up the web to the house of the Sun and left the jugs. Later, Mainu

climbed out, put the letter on a table, and hid. When the Sun arrived for a drink of water, he saw the letter and read it. "I, Kimana, a man of Earth, wish to marry your daughter."

Nobody could tell the Sun how the letter got there. So the Sun wrote a reply and again left it on the table. Mainu secretly took the letter, and when the jugs needed refilling with water, he returned to Earth.

Kimana read the letter and said to Mainu, "The Sun wants a purse of money as a wedding gift. How am I to do this if I cannot get to heaven?"

"I will take the purse for you," said Mainu.

Mainu returned to heaven with the purse. And so it was arranged for the daughter of the Sun and Moon to descend to Earth. Yet there was nobody to greet her.

"How am I to find my husband if he has not come to greet me?" she wondered.

"I will take you," said Mainu, looking out from the well.

"How can you, a frog, help me?"

"I brought you the letter and the money."

"Then it is you I shall marry," said the daughter. As for Kimana—he still awaits his bride.

The frog is an amphibian, which means it can live both in water and on land.

Arion and the Dolphin

This tale describes how a dolphin saved a musician in ancient Greece from drowning.

The renowned **lute** player Arion was returning by ship to his home in Corinth, Greece, from the port of Tarentum in southern Italy. He had just attended a musical competition in Sicily, which he had won. The sailors, seeing Arion's prizes of gold and jewels, plotted to kill him and steal the treasure.

"Hurl him into the sea," ordered the captain. "If anybody asks after him, we will say we never saw him fall overboard."

Dionysus, the god of wine, was once captured by pirates. They mistook him for a wealthy prince and thought they could hold him for ransom. After the ship set sail, the god used his powers to make vines overgrow the ship. He turned the oars into serpents that terrified the sailors into jumping into the sea. But then Dionysus took pity on the sailors. He turned them into dolphins, to spend their lives helping people in peril at sea.

When Arion realized his fate, he begged the sailors to let him play one last song on his lute. Aware of his reputation as a great musician, they agreed. Arion began to play knowing that dolphins, too, liked the sound of music.

The sailors were moved by his wonderful playing—but not enough to stop them from throwing him overboard. Arion splashed into the sea. The sailors were sure he would drown.

As Arion had hoped, his music attracted a dolphin. The creature saved his life by carrying him all the way to land. But, in the end, the effort of pulling Arion so far was too much. The poor dolphin died on the beach. To show his gratitude, Arion had a statue of the dolphin erected on that spot.

White Elephant

In this tale from India, a kindly elephant wishes only to look after his mother.

There once lived a magnificent and rare white elephant who had a kind-hearted soul. He lived near a lake by Mount Candorana with his mother, who was aged and blind. White Elephant looked after her with great care. He brought her fruits from the forest and cool water from the lake.

One day, White Elephant came across a **forester** who had been lost for days. He carried the forester on his back to a village. From there, the forester returned to his home in Benaras.

Soon after, the King of Benaras's personal elephant died. The king announced a huge reward for anyone who knew of an elephant magnificent enough to replace it.

The forester guided the king's soldiers to where White Elephant lived. On seeing them, White Elephant knew they had come for him. He realized that if he put up a struggle, many soldiers would be killed. So he decided to go quietly.

At Benaras, White Elephant was given his own stable and everything he desired. Yet he neither ate nor drank. The king was informed and went to see him.

"Why are you sulking so?" he asked. "Is it not a great honor to serve your king?"

"I can neither eat nor drink for worrying about my poor mother," replied White Elephant. "She is old and blind and has no one to take care of her."

The king was also kindly. Hearing this, he immediately released White Elephant so he could return to care for his mother.

Many years later, after White Elephant had died, the king erected a statue of him by the side of the lake. Every year, a fine elephant festival was held there, in memory of such a caring and noble soul.

Elephants in Asia have been used for centuries for war, hunting, transportation, and logging.

GLOSSARY

bragging Saying something in a boastful manner

composure Sense of calmness

diligent Showing great care in and attention to work or duties

domesticated Made an animal adapt to living around humans

forester A person responsible for managing the growth and use of forests

gourd A plant with a hard shell or outer casing. This can be hollowed out to make a vessel that holds water, such as a bowl or jug.

lute An early stringed instrument, similar to a guitar

mussels Shellfish similar to oysters, found in fresh and salt water

Proconsul Governor of a province in the ancient Roman Republic

trickster In folk tales of various cultures, an often mischievous hero who uses deception

INDEX